Uber Lift

Uber Lift by Robin Dosskey is a compelling story about two strangers who have a lot more in common with each other than first meets the eye. From the vantage point of having tragically lost her own son, Kyle, to the terrible disease of addiction, Robin Dosskey deftly weaves multiple insightful narratives throughout this "uber lift" of a story. All in all, *Uber Lift* is as moving as it is hopeful. It is a must-read for readers of all ages as it is very relevant for the times we are all living in today.

—SARAH ZELTSER, *Substance Use Disorder Counselor,*
The Geo Group

Robin Dosskey's *Uber Lift* is a tale full of wisdom, but as a literary achievement, it takes the reader on what can be best described as a wild, emotional ride. What kind of literature is it? In a sense it is a "short story," but a very long one—maybe a novella. But it is also a compilation of stories, weaving a mesmerizing series of fables within the story, each a compelling tale on its own, but all serving as suspenseful steps toward a profound climax.

As a reader one is drawn from the start into a vortex of altered space and time, descending into the very confused and tormented world of the addict: the one who suffers from substance use disorder. She draws you in to witness the fragility of the vulnerable human. Her goal is to help you understand how the addict desperately seeks peace, and in the end, she shouts from the rooftops to stop this senseless loss of life and potential.

Uber Lift, as the title suggests, begins innocuously in a series of almost random interactions between a driver—who is the tragic hero—and an older customer, who then slowly and mysteriously emerges as his spiritual godfather. The narrative of their relationship alternates with a sequence of metaphoric fables that illustrates the addict's journey and challenges. Each one goes deeper to another level, revealing human frailty and vulnerability. Taken one at a time, these fables keep the reader uncertain, with endings, some of which are vague, some inconclusive, some fanciful. This compelling structure captures the author's search to attempt to make sense of the senseless palpable. But as we learn at the very end, it has all been about her heart-rending effort to imagine a different outcome for the true protagonist of the story—her own late son, Kyle. Indeed, Robin has said that she intuited these stories from Kyle himself.

In that sense, she has transformed his profound loss into a plea to others. The better outcome she tries to imagine for Kyle is redeemed as a plea for a better outcome for others. As she writes in her afterword, her goal is "to give readers a glimpse into the hell of opioid use disorder." And she hopes that "the shock value will awaken readers to the reality of this epidemic." We all know friends and families who have anguished over their loved one's addiction.

This is a cautionary tale and a profound search for meaning, but it is also a plea and a love letter to her beloved son, Kyle, who had such talent and promise.

—SUSAN WEISBERG, LCSW,
Hospice of the Valley

UBER LIFT

At the Crossroads

A chance meeting, a perceptive passenger,

and the power of compassion

come together in this tale of redemption and recovery

in the face of addiction.

Robin Dosskey

Book design: Anne Dosskey
Illustration: Jim Smyth

for Kyle,

whose journey helps me to awaken

You cannot hinder someone's free will,

that's the first law of the

Universe, no matter what the decision.

E.A. Bucchianeri

Uber Ride

As soon as he spotted the old man waiting on the curb one block ahead, Rick pulled off and parked. He let down all the windows, set the fan on high, pulled a can of air freshener from the glove box, and sprayed the car interior. Quickly he checked his face in the rear-view mirror and wiped off a few smudges, then emptied ashes from the tray onto the street. Adjusting the sleeves of his plaid wool shirt, he donned his tweed cap and sunglasses and drove ahead to meet his rider. He pulled up in his white four-door Toyota Prius in front of a senior apartment complex on Monticello Circle.

Douglas Newton approached, waving his cell phone showing the Uber confirmation. A relic of the 1970s, he wore a black bomber jacket, polo shirt, and loafers. Rick wondered why his dark crew cut showed so little gray. He jumped out to open the rear passenger door for him.

"So, Mr. Newton, you're headed to San Jose this morning?"

"Yes, I have an appointment at the medical clinic." His voice had the raspy sound of a long-time smoker. The driver glanced back at the old man in the back seat. Sallow complexion, deep bags under his eyes, yet a gentle smile like that of a favorite uncle. A long silence began their half-hour commute.

"So, may I call you Rick?" Getting a nod, he continued, "Do you think you could wait a few minutes when we arrive, and then give me a ride back to Mountain View?"

Rick was fighting drowsiness. He tried to stretch his back in the driver's seat while he considered the request. It was early enough that he could still make it to his class at the community college by 9 AM. It would be easy money.

"Sure," he nodded. Cell phone navigation directed him to a nondescript government building, which he recognized was an extension of the county medical complex.

He's getting chemotherapy treatments, he guessed. He had given cancer patients rides out there before. Rick parked by the clinic side door, and Mr. Newton slowly shuffled his way inside. While he waited, Rick turned on the radio, then got out and stretched. The California winter sun was breaking through the cloud layer. Rick took a few deep breaths, filling his nostrils with the earthy smell of the rain-soaked pavement. He was dizzy, a bit nauseous. He slid back into the driver's seat and listened to a song on the radio,

> *While you smile on the outside*
> *You're screaming on the inside*
> *You inhale without breathing*
> *Talk without believing*
> *You're not running, only skidding*
> *Just trying to survive.*

He was nodding off when Mr. Newton returned moments later, startling him. Even worse, he insisted on joining him up front for the return ride. Rick felt particularly flustered to have his passenger up front, but Mr. Newton complained about the commute traffic, which put Rick at ease. By this time, commuter traffic was flooding onto Highway 280. The mad rush to beat the standstills had begun. Rick swerved to avoid a Lexus bulldozing into his lane without signaling.

"Look at that!" he muttered, "Guy thinks that he's entitled to the whole road!"

"Darn fools!" Mr. Newton replied, acknowledging the offense. As they chatted, the older man noted several burn holes on his driver's right jacket sleeve, and glancing down, a cigarette lighter in the coffee cup holder, but no butts in the ashtray. A "No Smoking" sign was clearly posted on the dashboard.

Upon arrival at Monticello Circle, Mr. Newton again thanked him and, while handing Rick a ten-dollar tip, asked, "I'm wondering if you could pick me up next Thursday, as well. Same time. I need ongoing treatments."

Rick removed his sunglasses to help the old man schedule his next Uber rideshare using his cell phone app. This time Mr. Newton caught a glimpse of dark circles beneath the young man's bloodshot eyes. They shook hands and Mr. Newton ambled off toward the apartment front steps.

He hesitated, turned around, and called back, "Oh, and please call me Douglas."

* * *

The following Thursday morning Douglas slowly eased his stiff body onto the front passenger seat, smiled, and greeted his driver.

"Morning, Rick."

Rick caught a strong whiff of Old Spice aftershave blended with cigarette smoke. Holding a manila envelope on his lap, Douglas set a small, black, leather case on the passenger floor and buckled himself in. Rick sped onto the freeway in a futile attempt to beat the commuters. The radio reported the last-second

Warriors loss to the Celtics. They both vented their disappointment. The drive itself was a series of spurts and slowdowns into San Jose. The scenic Highway 280 winds south into Santa Clara Valley through the hazy gray-green hills between the bay lands and craggy blue-violet Santa Cruz Mountains. Thousands of commuters file onto Highway 280, passing by miles of housing tracts and office buildings between the myriad of off-ramps cross-connecting the sprawling suburbia. Since Douglas had a captive listener, he volunteered a bit of his life.

"I grew up in Santa Clara Valley. I worked for electronic companies here until I retired. Now I'm enjoying a few hobbies. Cooking and writing fiction, in between clinic visits." He shifted the manila envelope on his lap.

Rick nodded as Douglas talked, but he was preoccupied. *He must be early in his course of chemo. He hasn't lost his hair.* Out of politeness, he didn't pry into the old man's illness. He wanted to finish the trip and get to class, then sleep and hopefully work on an assignment that was due.

Upon arrival at the medical clinic, Douglas struggled out of the car clutching his small, black case and the manila envelope.

"Okay, wait here, I'll be back in ten or fifteen minutes, tops," he instructed. Then leaning in through the passenger window he said, "Hey Rick, by any chance, do you like to read? Do you like stories? While you wait, would you mind reading my story?" With a grin he added, "It might be an entertaining way to kill time and I could use your feedback."

He handed Rick the envelope and ambled toward a clinic side door across the street. Rick shook his head. *An easy Uber job never turns out to be easy.* He wearily grabbed some gum, removed a manuscript from the envelope, and started to read. It was so short that he didn't bother to put on his glasses. He'd get through it quickly and appease Douglas. He needed the tip.

Longhorn

Way out in the American West on the open range lands a herd of Longhorn bovines roamed. Young Blaze Longhorn was having that feeling again. Was it dissatisfaction? Restlessness? Hopelessness? The herd was back on the trail, migrating south for the buffalo grass. Just like last year, and the year before that, and the one before that. Each year he had put on more weight, more muscle. Now his hide was thick with fur from his poll to his hocks and pasterns. His horns had lengthened, too, almost as long now as the old bulls'. Yes, he'd be ready to challenge the old bulls once they crossed the Red River and arrived at the resting corrals. Then he could claim his own cows and mate! He was daydreaming of his cows when he absently lifted one pastern to scratch himself.

"Feeling a bit itchy?" laughed an old heifer, chewing a clump of sand sage. "You've got to wait until you have more brains than testosterone!" she teased. Blaze snorted and stomped off to the side of the herd.

They're always mocking me, dumb cows! he fumed. *Someday I will lead the herd and they won't laugh.* The herd trotted ahead to reach a patch of prairie shortgrass. *Same old, same old tastes. No variety, ever,* he complained to himself. He noticed some new, different plants, taller and reddish-colored growing beneath the hoodoo rocks. He stretched for a muzzleful when, out of nowhere, he was butted backwards with thundering force. Blaze landed on his rump, humiliated.

"What the heck was that for?" he yelled, looking up to find Old Governor Bull glaring at him.

"You're a BOVINE!" he bellowed. With his left longhorn, he dug under the plant and tossed it, roots and all, into a sage thicket. "We don't eat that plant! It can kill you, and way before the humans do!" he added. "Of course, if you eat it, you'll die happy, kick-up-your-hooves happy, they say. Like I said, Young Bull, er, what's your name? Oh yeah, Blaze." Old Gov rambled on, "I knew your mother well. I believe she died of tick fever, right?" He was pawing at the turf and continued, "As a matter of fact, I'm probably your father. Anyways, don't eat that plant. You'd likely die." He galloped off, his muscular flanks rippling with sweat, having done his duty as the alpha bull should.

Blaze trudged along with the fifty head, all mooing and bellowing, sinking deeper into despair. The dust clouds made him cough, and he could barely see where they were going. His thirst was unbearable. His fetlocks hurt. Gadflies kept invading, stinging the corners of his eyes. Dusk had set in as they traveled the ridge. At least they could rest again, maybe find some mesquite branches to brush up against. A grove of juniper trees would be a pleasant wind break. Lord, how he hated this herd life! I'm meant to take over the herd. I'm smarter and stronger than all of them. As the herd settled down to rest in high pasture, the stars came out and the cattle lay down, heads lowering to sleep. Blaze found a spot to himself under a juniper tree.

"I'm taking the lead tomorrow!" he declared aloud, to no one, he thought.

"Good idea," a low voice purred. "I've been watching you.

You've got what it takes, all right." Blaze strained to see who was speaking. It wasn't a bovine voice.

"Up here, in the tree," the voice purred. It was a mangy mountain lion, stretched out on the thickest branch, eyes gleaming gold in the dark. Blaze gasped at the size of him, but quickly realized an attack was not imminent. The cat was outnumbered.

"As I was saying, 'You've got it, the strength and smarts to take the lead of the herd, but do you have the guts?'"

Now Blaze was curious, "What do you mean?"

"You lack confidence! You can't mope around as a leader. You have to make big, bold decisions."

How do I learn that, he asked himself. He *had* made a bold decision. He would not migrate another season to get his chance to lead. *Enough already!*

"I know how you can get courage," the cat continued, casually licking a paw, claws extended. "It's simple. See the shrub along the ridge there, a ways from the grass? Red color with the seed pods? Take a few mouthfuls. You'll have your confidence in no time at all."

Blaze hesitated, then shook his head, "Governor Bull said not to eat that. It's poisonous."

"Of course, he'd tell you that. He doesn't want you to change. He wants to keep you in your place, just another weakling bull in the herd." The mountain lion licked the fur on his chest, then yawned, stretched, and rose up on the branch.

"Excuse me, I don't want to wake the herd, so I'll just take my leave down the trail. Let's pretend this conversation never happened. Happy trails to you … for the rest of your miserable life." He leapt off the branch, bounding down the hill in the moonlight.

Without making a rustle, Blaze cautiously approached the forbidden plant.

I could try a mouthful, then make my way to the front of the herd, and take the lead at dawn. Just need a bit of courage, he thought. He tore off a pod and chewed slowly, knowing full well the herb was snaking its way through all four chambers of his bovine stomach by the warming sensation in his gut. Moments later he violently threw up the cud.

I poisoned myself! he thought, in a panic. But then, like a wave, the euphoria came on. For hours, it was a heart-pounding, hoof-stomping bliss! King-of-the-mountain exhilaration!

At dawn, he stood on the canyon rim and bellowed at the herd, "Get up, you lazy beasts and follow me! I'm showing you where the sweetest buffalo grass is!" The aroused herd slowly rose on their hooves, stretched and began to move, just like any other day. Blaze snorted and charged ahead, adrenaline coursing through him. The herd picked up pace to follow. Shortly, Blaze lunged forward into a full gallop. Now, in stampeding confusion, they followed him.

Right over the cliff.

The mountain lion watched from above until the dust clouds finally cleared, surveying the size of the herd lying dead or twitching on the canyon floor. He made his way down the boulders to feast. Of course, he'd have to share with the bobcats, coyotes, and vultures. Works every time! Young bovine stupidity.

*   *   *

Rick broke into a laugh, then almost choked on his gum. He stuffed the story back in the envelope. What could he say to the old guy? At least he was enjoying his hobby. He removed his cap and rubbed his temples, fighting his headache. Douglas returned, slid himself into the front seat along with his small black case.

"Well, did you read my western? What did you think?" That's

when he noticed the purple goose egg on Rick's forehead, but made no comment.

"I'd say, truthfully, it's a very superficial western. No cowboys and no shootouts. More of a fable, but not as good as Aesop's." He felt bad saying it, but he was expected to honestly critique it. He apologized, adding, "On the other hand, my critique might be influenced by my headache. I tripped and fell on the apartment steps last night."

"Maybe you should get checked out for a concussion." Douglas chose his reply carefully, to not comment too much.

"Nah, I already slept and woke up. I'm okay."

Returning to the book review, Douglas replied, "Well your assessment is brutally honest, but I'm going to keep writing. It's discouraging, but I should improve." Raising his eyebrows, he added, "Listen, Rick, I've just had an idea. Would you continue giving me an Uber lift every Thursday morning? I'll even sweeten the deal each time with a fifteen-dollar cash tip."

Rick thought it through. He needed cash. Sure, he could make better tips by driving the business travelers to San Francisco, but it would be less traffic stress to San Jose. This was guaranteed income. He accepted with a nod.

"So, what is your favorite western of all time?" Douglas asked him on the drive back.

"It would have to be *Shane* by Schaefer, a masterpiece, an original. What's yours?"

"*The Good, the Bad, and the Ugly*. I liked the theme music."

"Seriously?" Rick scoffed. "That wasn't a novel, just a spaghetti western!"

"So, you do read literature."

"Yes, when I can't relax and fall asleep, my bed partner is my loyal Kindle."

He flashed back to reading novels in bed with Gemma, taking

turns to read the chapters aloud. Debates about each character's motives inevitably followed. He missed her soulful reactions. Still, it was much easier falling asleep with a Kindle. The Kindle didn't have issues with him in the morning.

As soon as he had dropped Douglas back at Monticello Circle and received his tip, Rick sped off to class, trying not to think about stoned bulls.

*   *   *

The clouds were aglow with a golden, rose-tinged light of dawn the following Thursday. Rick was already waiting out in front of the apartments at Monticello Circle. Not that he looked forward to the drive, but he had committed to the work and wanted to finish fast. They greeted each other. Douglas took a last drag off his cigarette, crushed the butt on the pavement, then climbed onto the front seat. Glancing down he noted ashes in the utility tray. Sunglasses masked Rick's eyes.

On the drive to the hospital, they bemoaned the 49ers' loss on Monday night. Douglas asked if he had family in the area. Rick shook his head. Did he play sports? He used to play rugby, but injured his shoulder, so he quit. And no girlfriend? He had one, but they had broken up.

"She couldn't tolerate my bad habits," Rick shared, without getting specific. "Like I said, I like to read good literature for relaxation, because I don't sleep well. I had to give up a stressful job in tech sales. Now I'm taking a technical writing course, so I don't have a lot of free time. Sometimes I hang out with friends, have a beer, watch a game. I try to sleep in on the weekends." He hoped this would appease Douglas's curiosity.

"When I was in my forties I had a back injury from a car accident," Douglas shared. "The doctors put me on painkillers. It helped me sleep, but probably too much." He glanced up to read Rick's reaction. Deadpan expression.

Just as before, Douglas handed Rick the worn manila envelope, this time a bit stained with coffee rings. "Could you please read the new one? It's a fairy tale." He didn't wait for a response. "See you in ten minutes."

Rick hesitated, wondering what Douglas might say if he *didn't* read it. Feeling a sense of resolve, he cracked his knuckles and began to read. The cash tip was worth it, sort of.

Fairy Tale

It's always the same daydream because it works so well—anywhere. Like when you sleep in on Saturday morning, or zone out in math or poli sci class.

You're in a golden field, wearing a long white linen dress, a wreath of baby roses in your hair, watching, waiting. In the distance, galloping toward you on a white stallion is a prince. He's ruggedly handsome and strong. As his horse halts, the prince swoops you up with him and away you gallop to his palace. Not the ostentatious one, but the small castle that's hidden in the mist across the lake. He'll row you across the lake, his gaze of love enveloping your being. You'll dance in the ballroom for hours, his embrace acknowledging you with honor and respect, declaring his love for you, body and soul. No words are needed. You climb the winding staircase to the bedchamber and sink together in the goose down bed, his touch as gentle as the lake water lapping on the shore. All night you're in each other's arms, gazing at the view of the azure lake and the Milky Way floating above it.

The teacher drones on about supply and demand. You couldn't care less.

At three o'clock, you're off campus responding to cell texts, checking Snapchat. You bike home, wolf down a bagel, and head to soccer practice. Every night you'll replay the daydream to fall asleep.

But the dream takes on a life of its own.

Back in the castle, you awaken to find your prince gone, off to conquer an enemy in the north. He's left you a note in beautiful script on parchment, reaffirming his devotion and love. He promises to return as soon as the battle is won, perhaps in a few days or weeks.

Alone in the castle, you wait, wondering when he will return. Days become weeks, weeks turn into months, months become a year. You scan the lake, hoping for his approach. Has he died in battle? If he lives, what battle scars will he have? Will he even recognize you?

One day, you decide to ride north to search for him. But first you will have to find a horse and provisions. You will need a guide and a map. You will bring herbs and medicines in case he is ill or wounded. You will need to wait for the spring thaw, as the high mountain road is treacherous when it's covered with ice and snow.

Months later, you have finally embarked, climbed through the mountain pass, and crossed into a foreign land. There is a weathered wooden sign on the road. "Oracle Pond," it reads. There is an old, old man in a hooded robe. He is silently pointing farther down the road. He seems to indicate that going down that road will take all your courage. You take a deep breath and urge your horse onward. He is snorting then trotting, then halting, spinning, uneasy with the surroundings, ears perked, nervously pacing through the woods to reach an open meadow. He suddenly halts, rears up, and you see why. Branches poke from the ground. No, they are stick crosses. You soothe the horse and dismount, slowly approaching a makeshift grave, heart pounding.

He has reappeared, that ancient man, just standing, silently.

You gulp, your voice quavering, "Whose grave is this, sir?"

He responds, "Soldier's grave ... from a country to the south ... an unknown prince." With that sudden realization, you sink down by the grave, the sadness crushing your entire being.

"Did he die bravely in battle?" you ask.

Ancient One waves a wrinkled hand and gives you a vision. He shows you that the prince had died before the battle had even begun. He had quenched his thirst from Oracle Pond and had seen his true self in the reflection. He died fighting the enemy of his own mind.

"What enemy could he possibly have in his mind?" you ask in your anguish. "That he was not brave, not strong? That he did not love himself?" You clench your fists, collapse on the grassy mound and sob, tears falling on his grave.

You make the long painful journey home, reflecting on the moments you shared with your prince, still feeling his love enveloping you, grieving, reflecting, wondering why. After months of riding, you finally arrive at the castle, eerily empty by the lake shrouded in fog. By then you've decided. Home will no longer be that castle. You lock it up with the heavy iron key, throw the key into the lake, and ride away.

*　　*　　*

Rick smirked, rubbed his eyes, and stuffed the manuscript back in the envelope. *Gemma would have liked it. Women want a prince to sweep them off their feet and give them attention, night and day.* He flashed back to their first summer together, picnics by the lake, reading poetry to her on the blanket,

> I will arise and go now, and go to Innisfree,
> And a small cabin build there of clay and wattles made;

"What are wattles?" she asked, turning over on her back.

He brushed a wisp of hair off her lips. "A kind of fencing." He read on,

And I shall have some peace there, for peace comes dropping slow,
Dropping from the veils of the morning to where the cricket sings;

"So where is Innisfree?" she interrupted.

"It's the Isle of Innisfree in Lough Gill, Ireland, where Yeats spent his summers."

"Take me there someday," she smiled.

"OK, if you let me finish his poem. And let me kiss you a thousand times first."

*   *   *

A car alarm went off in the clinic parking lot, interrupting his daydream. But Rick needed to get out and stretch. He leaned against the car, letting the sun warm his face, warm like Gemma's sweet kisses used to feel. He got back in the car.

True to his word, Douglas tapped on the driver's window signaling, "Okay, ready to go." He climbed into the front seat with his black case, a look of surprise on his face.

"You read it? What did you think?" he asked.

Rick thought maybe he should politely lie. But on second thought, it would be kinder to break it to him early; he's no writer.

"It's sort of a fairy tale, written for a girl, with a sad ending. Fairy tales should end 'happily ever after.' I'm sorry, Douglas, but I don't think this is your genre either. Why not research some classics and develop a theme? You know, something like 'good wins over evil.'"

"Good doesn't always win over evil."

"Maybe not, but it makes for a great story."

"What is your favorite fairy tale?"

Rick pondered it. "I was always intrigued by *Pinocchio*. At the end, the puppet becomes a real boy."

"And the puppet maker loved him unconditionally, even when he lied. So, he learned to be authentic."

Rick nodded, "Yeah, that too."

Acceleration

The following Thursday, Douglas waited patiently in the gray light of early morning until Rick arrived, almost twenty minutes late. He had his suspicions, but his plan did not require confrontations.

"Hey Douglas, I'm really sorry, man! I didn't hear the alarm and overslept."

Douglas dismissed the late arrival with a wave and promptly handed Rick another manuscript. "You owe me this."

Rick emphatically shook his head, "Hey, Douglas, you should take a creative writing class, get some expert guidance. I'm just an Uber driver," he said. "I can't help you with creative writing."

Douglas took a final drag of his cigarette and threw it down the gutter grate. "I'm really trying to quit, you know," he said as he lowered himself into the Prius.

Douglas wasn't going to give Rick the chance to refuse. "Listen, Rick," choosing his words carefully, "actually, you are helping me find my forte. Could you please just read this new one? Different genre, more of a contemporary teen story."

Arriving at the destination, Douglas gestured a "wait here" over his shoulder as he headed into the clinic. He was thinking about the red rash that had erupted on Rick's face, like he'd been stung by ten wasps. He wouldn't press him about it. Not yet. His was a delicate strategy.

Inside the clinic, Douglas flashed back to his own life fifteen years before, a desperate man gripped in pain. He had survived and walked the razor's edge. Reflecting on how Rick was starting to look like a smallpox victim, he realized he'd need to speed things up.

Rick watched the old man amble into the clinic, then, reluctantly, began to read his next manuscript.

The Proposal

One afternoon you're trudging home from school. Your backpack is loaded with textbooks. If only the bike hadn't had a flat tire this morning, you'd be riding home. Get down this boulevard and five more blocks. Jeez, your back aches, so you set the backpack down for a bit on the sidewalk. There's a young woman, about thirty years old, in a lounge chair on her front lawn enjoying a smoothie. She's beautiful—long blond hair, flashing dark eyes, and clear skin. She smiles and greets you. "You must be tired! Pull up a chair for a minute," she invites you. You sit down and look more closely. She's dressed like a model, right out of *Elle* magazine—four-hundred dollar boots, a silk blouse, and leather jacket. She's wearing a silver chain and a pendant that looks like a Celtic design.

"Have a soda," she offers, pointing to the cooler on the lawn. You grab a bottle and gulp it down while she starts talking.

"I bet you're in high school." You nod. She shakes her head and grins. "That's tough. I think too much pressure is put on kids here. Got to make the grade and get into UC. It feels like you're never good enough." She takes a sip of her drink and continues, "Maybe you didn't make the team, you don't qualify for the AP class, can't afford a car yet, and all your friends have one." You nod and finish off the soda.

"And to make matters worse, you have to worry about friends. Do they really like you, or are they going to talk about you on social media?" You nod emphatically. You're thinking she knows a thing or two.

"Are you a counselor?" you ask, holding back a burp.

"No, not really, but I do help people. I've been in your place, not so long ago." She sweeps back hair from her face, long, manicured nails gleaming pearlescent white, and continues in a low volume. "I can help, but it depends on how motivated you are. I can make things go differently."

"Yeah, with magic?" you joke.

She grins wide. "Actually, yes, but this isn't for everybody, just for the brave—some healing, relaxing energy." She leans forward. "Seriously, I can give you the power to change your life." She's reading your expression.

Okay, she's a religious freak, you're thinking.

"You can have an experience that will instantly change your whole outlook for the better."

"That would be a miracle," you say, smirking.

"Miracles do happen," she explains, reading your mind. "Of course, it does cost a little for this supplement. It is my business." Oh, you get it now; *she's into a startup business with health supplements, protein powder, hence the ice chest. She's going to sell you some protein shake mix. Ugh!* You hastily decline and say goodbye as you grab your backpack.

"Late, gotta go!" you tell her. She holds out her hand to have you shake it. She's wearing a gaudy fake emerald ring, in putrid green.

"Well, okay," she replies, still clasping your hand. "Not ready yet, but I've given you a sample. Hey, my name's Annamarie, but friends call me Maya." She lets go. "If you change your mind, I'm here, but not on the weekends."

As you stride home, you're thinking it strange, because you don't recollect her handing you a sample. Though that bottle of soda did taste a little off …

Once home, you throw down your backpack and stretch out on your bed. You should study for the algebra test, but you're just too tired. Tired of everything. You ache from jogging in PE and walking home with the heavy backpack. Always a stomachache before the tests. And so tired. Never sleeping well. You can't fall asleep most nights. Then when you finally do fall asleep in the morning, you're late to school. Right now, you just want to crash for a while, so you drift off. You dream that Maya's standing there on the lawn with soothing words.

"Rest now. No more worries."

And sleep you do, for several hours, dreaming in heavenly peace of serene worlds where there's no pain, no competition, no betrayal, no struggle. You wake to the smell of a pot roast dinner wafting from the kitchen and you sit up in bed and stretch. Nothing hurts and there's nothing to worry about. You flash back to a time when you were just a little kid, when a nap before dinner was all you had to do, your day was timeless, and you belonged to this warm and cozy home. It felt so right. You feel blessed and peaceful, all night.

Until the next morning. You're achy and depressed, even worse than usual. You didn't study, so now you're screwed on the math test. You think maybe you'll stop by and ask Maya what that supplement is called. You might buy a trial packet.

*   *   *

Rick turned the last page several times looking for an additional page. He shook his head, frowning in disapproval. Bright sunshine had already burst through the foggy marine layer hanging over the valley. He stuffed the pages back in the envelope and stepped out of the Prius to cool off. He was sweating and his body rash was itching. Douglas promptly returned, climbing into the front seat.

"Well? Is this one on track?" He searched Rick's face for his reaction.

"Too confusing!" Rick snapped. "Why didn't you explain what it was that made him high?"

"Does it matter what made him high?" Douglas answered. "The point is, he felt really good being high."

"So why didn't you write an ending? It's too frustrating, leaving the reader dangling like that." Rick banged his fist on the dashboard.

"Isn't the ending obvious?" Douglas asked.

"No," Rick erupted, "it isn't because he had a choice to make."

"Yay! I got your hackles up with this story. I am a bit pleased with myself!"

"It was incomplete."

"All right, I'll try harder on the next one," Douglas promised.

*   *   *

Rick was punctual the following week, even early. His sleep cycle was completely off. At 6:35 AM, Douglas again approached the Prius, waved, then took several drags on his cigarette before tossing it down, as usual. He inched onto the front seat, and, as if setting down an IED, gently laid the envelope on the seat. Rick frowned at the sight of the envelope and shook his head in protest.

"I know, I know, no more stories!" Douglas laughed. "But look!" he exclaimed holding up a bag and cup. "I've brought you coffee and a giant oatmeal raisin cookie to sweeten the deal!" He searched Rick's expression. "How about it? Hey, this one's a hor-ror story. Don't you like horror stories? Enjoy!"

When they reached the clinic, Rick rudely snatched the man-uscript and the cookie bag, and Douglas headed off to the clinic side door. Rick tip took a sip of coffee and began to read.

The Trial

The trial was held at the Redwood City Superior Courthouse, in the 1930s-era courtroom on the third floor. One could smell the antique varnished oak floors. In the front center was a massive elevated oak desk for the judge, with two rows of jury seats, full of jurors, to the left of the judge. The witness box below the judge's bench was now empty. The trial had been going on for several days and most witnesses had finished testifying.

Judge Curtner pounded his gavel. "The trial of Derrick Chase vs. San Mateo County continues. We will now hear from the prosecution." He looked at the prosecuting attorney.

"Mr. Manley, present your case."

Manley stood and faced the courtroom. "Please bring in Exhibit A."

A cart, contents covered with a white sheet, was wheeled in front of the judge's dais.

"Members of the court, I will show you the extent of Mr. Chase's crimes." When he removed the sheet, the courtroom gallery gasped.

"This is a model of Mr. Chase's brain." Using a laser pen, he pointed to spots on the brain. "Look at the damage caused by opioid abuse. Notice the back area of the cerebral cortex with these thin wires. Ladies and gentlemen, that is unnatural! His brain has been completely rewired by his addiction! He was not born this way. Mr. Chase has caused this!"

The defense attorney scrambled to his feet, shouting, "We object, Your Honor!"

Judge Curtner replied, "Proceed."

The defense attorney asked for the laser pen, and then, stepping up to the model of the brain, explained, "I want the court to understand the true cause of Mr. Chase's actions. May we have the courtroom lights dimmed please?" The judge motioned to continue.

In the dim light the defense attorney began, "Serotonin is a chemical in the brain. It is necessary to calm a person's anxiety and to help him sleep. In dim light it will show up as a fluorescent blue. I ask the court, 'Do you see fluorescent blue in this brain?'"

Judge Curtner shook his head. "That is because there is so little of it! What we see is a white brain, devoid of serotonin. Mr. Chase had been trying to rebalance the levels of serotonin in his brain his entire life. Had he had expert psychiatric care, he might have had serotonin rebalanced with medications."

The prosecuting attorney retaliated, "Objection! Your Honor, Mr. Chase did not seek psychiatric treatment on a regular basis. He alone began his addiction. Once he rewired his brain, he spent his life coping with his illicit drug needs, causing the cycle of drug abuse and dishonesty, leading to fraud, theft, abandonment of his health, his family, friends, and his career. He must be held accountable. We rest our case."

The judge turned to the jury, "You are dismissed to begin your deliberations."

The jury slowly filed out of the room, returning in less than an hour.

The judge asked, "Jury, what is your verdict?"

The presiding juror stood to face the judge. "We find the defendant, Derrick Chase, guilty on all counts, Your Honor: abuse, negligence, abandonment, theft, and fraud. We request justice to the full extent of the law."

"The jury's verdict has been recorded." Then, turning to the defendant he said, "The defendant will rise. Does the defendant wish to make a statement before sentencing?" Derrick Chase rose humbly and faced the judge, shoulders slumped, beginning to speak in a quavering voice.

"Your Honor, I admit to having made very bad choices. I let down my guard but only hoped to find relief from the emotional crisis I was in. I see now that my choices took me down a path of physical and emotional ruin." He broke down sobbing, "I harmed myself, my family, and my community. I beg you, give me one more chance to reclaim a normal life." He paused, adding, "I promise to fulfill all of the requirements of my incarceration and rehabilitation. I am truly sorry. I only wish to make amends while I serve out the sentence."

Judge Curtner nodded that he had heard and understood. "I will proceed with the sentencing." He scanned the room, making eye contact with the jurors, the visitors, and the defendant, then somberly announced:

"The defendant, Derrick Chase, has been found guilty of committing the crimes of abuse, negligence, abandonment, theft, and fraud." He paused to let that sink in. "From the testimony, we can accept that his errors in judgment were not premeditated. However, the initial crime against himself was consciously committed, and it led to the multiple offenses impacting himself and society. The defendant will now stand for sentencing." Hushed silence followed.

Looking squarely at the defendant he declared, "Derrick Chase, you have admitted your guilt and have sincerely apologized to this court. You have demonstrated a willingness to rehabilitate, and this court accepts your sincerity to make amends. However, through your own actions over the course of your addiction, you must realize that the damage to your brain is extensive. Furthermore, since the heroin use has rewired your brain, your judgment is clouded by your physical addiction and emotional pain, so a typical course of incarceration, rehabilitation, and probation will not suffice." The judge paused so the court recorder could catch up.

"Your sentence actually began years ago with the self-imposed confinement you already experience within your mind. You will be offered professional therapy and basic health care. There is no medication known to cure this illness of addiction. Employment must be put on hold. You will be allowed visitations by your family and friends, but you will not be able to participate in activities with them due to your diminished emotional state and physical health." The judge frowned and leaned toward the defendant. "Be vigilant, as your mind will continually interrupt your peace, and you will want to suppress it every hour of every day." He sternly warned, "You must never abuse your brain again or your actions may prove fatal." He wasn't finished.

"Hence, rehabilitation will be up to you, with the help that is offered and the resources you choose to utilize," the judge continued. "You alone hold the keys to release yourself from your prison. In a moment of clarity, you may wish to kneel down to thank the universe for its love and mercy, and by accepting all spiritual and professional help available, you may reclaim your life from your addiction. Have you understood the sentence as presented?"

Derrick Chase lowered his head, "I have, Your Honor."

Judge Curtner pounded his gavel. "Case closed." The pounding echoed in Derrick's brain as the judge departed to his chambers. Derrick, handcuffed, was escorted through the courtroom side door, to the prison of his own creation.

*   *   *

Rick stopped munching the cookie. He set the manuscript down, rolling his eyes. He's losing it. He felt hot. He was sweating, but wearing only a t-shirt, he didn't dare peel off his hoodie.

Douglas returned. Rick handed back the envelope, shaking his head. "This one is really out there, I mean, a bit frightening, but, sorry, not a very entertaining story."

"Why not?"

"There should be an alien abduction, or a haunting, or murder."

"No, it isn't gory, but I think I made it horrifying. I was going for a *Dante's Inferno* effect."

"I suggest you read *The Shining*. Now that's a horror story!"

"I disagree. Not all horror stories have psychos or killings. The guy's mind was haunting him."

Douglas pointed out some black soot marks on Rick's face.

Rick quickly rubbed his face to dismiss them. The soot marks, he explained, were grease spots. He had just checked under the hood for an engine issue.

Rick just shook his head and continued, "I just didn't get the story. A guy doesn't harm his own brain on purpose. He shouldn't be punished for it."

"It happens all too often," Douglas muttered. He let out a sigh. "Well, I was hoping you'd feel the horror, but I guess everyone's idea of scary is different." Rick tried to object, but Douglas interrupted, "Hey, do you like double chocolate brownies? With walnuts? I've got an idea for a better horror story. I'll bring it next week."

Rick really hoped there wouldn't be another horror story. But there was.

Wheel of Intensity

"Welcome back folks, to *Wheel of Intensity*, the ultimate reality game show! Please welcome our next contestant, Mr. Ethan Mitchell." The audience applauds as Ethan steps forward into the stage spotlight and waves. "Ethan Mitchell is a resident of Sunnyvale, California. He's a UC Davis graduate with a specialized career. Ethan can you tell our audience what your career entails?"

Ethan keeps it brief, as he was coached, "I'm a paralegal law clerk."

The announcer continues, "As you know Ethan, in our show, *Wheel of Intensity*, each player has the opportunity to win the experience of a lifetime, just by spinning the ... Wheel ... of ... Intensity!" The audience cheers and whistles in anticipation.

"Calm down, audience, we need to go over the rules." He turns to Ethan, "Now, Ethan, you fully understand this is a game of chance, only for the brave?" Ethan nods and smiles politely. "And you realize, you have a chance to win a fabulous prize, which could be one hundred thousand dollars or a new car. But there's no changing your mind once you spin?"

"I understand," he says.

"Great, Mr. Mitchell, because some experiences of intensity

are anticipated, and you must know that there are risks to participating in this game, and the audience will be entertained as you play our game. Okay-y-y, so let's SPIN ... THE ... WHEEL OF INTENSITY!" The audience chants along. Ethan steps forward and spins the giant wheel, eight feet in diameter with blinking colored lights. The ticking arrow slows to a stop, and the audience waits in hushed silence.

"Well, Ethan, it looks like you did *not* win the hundred thousand dollars." The audience groans. "But, you do get an extra chance to win by picking something from behind our curtains!" The crowd erupts in applause.

"What will it be, Ethan? Curtain number one, curtain number two, or curtain number three?" A drum roll begins as Ethan glances at the curtains, then shuts his eyes.

"I'm going to take curtain number two!"

"Very good, Ethan!" Music plays and the announcer continues, "First, let's see what you *didn't* win. Show us curtain number one." The curtain opens to show a young family inside a bright red SUV. "Looks like you gave up the all-new Chevrolet Tahoe complete with the family of three! Looks like you won't be enjoying family time with a wife, son, and daughter at the beach or camping trips in the Sierras!" The audience groans in disappointment. Ethan shifts nervously.

"Now, let's see what Ethan didn't win behind curtain number three!" The curtain opens to reveal a poster-size cruise ship boarding pass and a beautiful background photo of an exotic tropical isle.

"Oh, gosh! Look at that, Ethan! You gave up the adventure of a lifetime—an all-expenses paid cruise to French Polynesia on the Grand Duchess Cruise Line, stopping at ten different islands before arriving at your own private bungalow in Tahiti!"

Ethan's head hangs low, playing the loser role, and the crowd groans again.

"Ethan, you chose curtain number two." Drumbeats roll as the announcer calls, "Please open curtain number two for Ethan!" The curtain opens to reveal a hospital bed. The audience in hushed whispers tries to anticipate what he'll get. Ethan's eyes grow wide.

"Well, Ethan, my friend, it looks like your *Wheel of Intensity* experience will be a bit different. You're going to experience heroin withdrawal!" He motions for the audience to clap. Light clapping starts as Ethan recoils in disbelief.

"Your experience starts as you are prescribed narcotic morphine-based painkillers for a knee injury." The crowd chuckles and Ethan, trying to appease the crowd, shrugs his shoulders and rolls his eyes. "But that's not all! No! Please bring out the tray." The show hostess strolls across the stage in a full-length, sequined cocktail dress, holding out the tray for Ethan to see, while the camera zooms in for a close-up shot. She sweeps her hand over various instruments.

"Once your prescription runs out and won't be refilled, you'll desperately try any street drug as a substitute! Oh yes! You will have all this paraphernalia at your disposal: pipes, glass vials, lighters, and syringes. You'll experiment with all these drug samples until you settle on the granddaddy of them all—heroin!"

The crowd cheers loudly. "But that's just the beginning!" The announcer throws up his arms in excitement. "Now, in full-blown addiction, you'll discover the intense experience of heroin withdrawal!" Now the audience roars with excitement, and Ethan crumbles to the stage floor.

"Oh, we know we picked the right contestant in you, Ethan, because you're stubborn and brave!" The man smiles widely, continuing, "You're going to need all your courage because your withdrawal is going to last a full eight weeks! Yes, you'll feel like you have the worst flu you ever experienced, and it won't let up!

You'll vomit and have the runs! You'll feel like a thousand spiders are crawling under your skin! Everything is going to hurt, even combing your hair," he exclaims. "You're going to have weeks of feeling paranoia, anger, and insomnia! And just when your physical symptoms subside, the real trouble begins. We will tag your brain with a memory chip so you will never forget that first feeling of pure, heavenly heroin ecstasy."

Ethan shakes his head, "Oh, God. No!"

"Oh, yes, Ethan! You will fight this compulsion for life! Congratulations, young man! Thanks for playing ... audience help me here ..."

"WHEEL ... OF ... INTENSITY!"

Ethan bolted upright in bed, sweat pouring from his forehead. Shaking, he exhaled a sigh of relief as his wife turned over, hoarsely whispering, "Another nightmare, honey?"

"Yeah, that's all," he replied and rose quickly to take a shower.

* * *

Rick tossed the manuscript envelope onto Douglas's lap. "This one's pretty scary, but as usual, why doesn't it have an ending?"

Douglas shook his head. "I thought the ending was obvious," he replied.

* * *

Douglas was waiting on the curb the following Thursday, ready to push his next, new manuscript on Rick. "I really hope you approve of this one," he confided. "Enjoy!"

Rick muttered a mild obscenity and grabbed the envelope. He chomped a bite of the brownie from the bag left for him on the seat once Douglas exited the car. He was feeling awful. He really needed that sugar boost and the fifteen-dollar tip. He had to rush back to town on an errand as soon as he dropped Douglas off. For now, he began to read.

The Suitcase

Alicia McCarthy was human resources director at Digital Design Corporation. All of the staff loved and trusted her, so it was no surprise when Sandy Richards tapped on her office door one late afternoon.

"Sandy! What can I do for you?" she asked, pushing back the desk chair to focus on the young woman. Clutching her backpack, Sandy sat down quickly and set a suitcase on the floor beside her.

"I need to take a leave of absence. Without pay, of course. How does that work?"

"Oh, sorry to hear that," Alicia replied. "Shall we call it personal necessity?" she suggested, not wanting to pry.

Sandy nodded.

"Employees have the option of up to three weeks without pay, but you'd have to be let go if you're away longer than that."

"All right, I can't say how long this will take, but I have to go out of town, up to Seattle, see some family there." Sandy glanced away nervously. She hastily signed the leave of absence form. Standing up to go, she stammered, "Alicia, can I ask a favor?"

Alicia nodded.

"Would you store my suitcase here with you? I'm catching a

plane in two hours, and just found out I have to pay for a second bag. I don't have time to drop it back home, and this is extra clothing I can live without."

Alicia smiled, "No problem. Been there, done that!" The suitcase was set aside by the personnel files.

Three weeks later, Sandy Richards officially gave notice by voicemail. Her phone number had been deactivated, her final paycheck automatically deposited. She left no forwarding address. After two months, Alicia decided to drop the suitcase at the nearest Goodwill center, but she planned to check through the contents first for any correspondence that might give her a way to contact Sandy.

At dinner that night, Alicia told the suitcase story to her husband, Josh, and their dinner guest, her brother-in-law, Gabe. She excused herself, going to bed early.

Josh called back to her, "So, should I take a look in the suitcase?" She told him to go ahead. She'd still take the contents to Goodwill on Saturday. It was a cheap, black fabric suitcase, without even rolling wheels. Josh and Gabe began to rummage through it. They found well-worn, pilled casual sweaters and leggings from Dollar Market, a photo of a young man, a pair of barely worn spike heels and a fake leather shoulder bag with a frayed strap. No letters, nothing written.

"Nothing worth saving," Josh commented. "Better check the purse."

The shoulder bag was empty except for the zippered inside pocket, which felt a bit soft.

Gabe reached inside, slowly removing a clear baggie. "Now, what do we have *here!*" he grinned. In this day and age, the white powder might be a drug, but what? Cocaine? Heroin? There was only one way to find out. And so they did, each licking a finger and tasting.

"Pretty sure it's heroin," Gabe surmised, as they both put a pinch on the back of their hands and this time sniffed it up into their nostrils. Ten minutes later a wave of nausea hit, both men rushing to the back lawn where they retched, then lay on the grass, laughing and, soon, swimming in euphoria.

"I think I just hugged an angel," said Josh.

For the first time in his life, Josh felt deep peace in his brain. He had never felt at home in his own skin. Years of trial prescriptions for anxiety and depression and painkillers for a back injury were like aspirin compared to this ambrosia.

"We cannot let this go to waste," declared Josh in a hushed tone. And they didn't. Getting together nightly, each took several small pinches at a time to get high, until one week later the bag was empty. By Sunday night, Josh was feeling sick, feeling like the worst flu he'd ever had. He called Gabe, and they commiserated.

After a very long silence, Josh said, "I think we need to find a guy."

*   *   *

Rick set the manuscript on his lap and took a sip of coffee, already gone cold. He was thinking that Douglas had been around the block himself. One had to know about drugs to write about such things.

"They don't call it heroin now," he informed Douglas when he returned to the car. "They call it junk, or black tar, or white stuff, and they smoke it or use a needle, I think."

"Probably so," admitted Douglas. "I had the idea for this story a very long time ago."

The return Uber ride was uncomfortably silent. Silent, as if a horrific secret had been revealed. Like they had stumbled upon a shallow, hastily dug grave, and human bones were jutting out of the dirt. Rick imagined his foot kicking soil to cover up the bones. *Why uncover stuff that needs to stay buried?*

He drove on, focused on the gridlocked freeway traffic, and began tapping out a rhythm on the dashboard to the tune on the radio. He was restless, not wanting to miss the turnoff. Douglas didn't ask for feedback on his story, but out of the blue, Rick volunteered it anyway.

"This last story held my interest a bit. I guess realistic fiction is more your talent."

He yawned. "I wish it had an ending. You really need to write an ending. You're not good with endings," he shared honestly.

"Oh, there's an ending," Douglas replied, "Oh yes, I haven't quite worked it out yet, but thanks." After a long period of silence, Douglas asked, "So what's your favorite novel?"

"*Ulysses*, by James Joyce." Rick swerved out of the slow lane as a truck merged onto the highway.

Douglas shook his head in dismay, "I tried reading it. I got lost in Joyce's complex narrative structure!"

Rick cleared his throat and recited:

Every life is in many days, day after day. We walk through ourselves, meeting robbers, ghosts, giants, old men, young men, wives, widows, brothers-in-love, but always meeting ourselves.

He gave his passenger a serious look. "Try to read it, Douglas. That's the kind of writing you should aim for."

As Douglas left the car he noted a nasty burn blister above Rick's lip, but restrained himself from asking about it. "See you next week," he called back. Rick sped off to run his errands.

The following week Douglas was waiting on the curb at Monticello Circle in the drizzling rain, wearing a ratty black raincoat and attempting to finish his cigarette without getting it wet.

He was shivering when he climbed into the passenger seat with his black case and manuscript.

"Thanks for the ride, again. Can you turn up the heat for me? I need to ask, can you hang around an extra fifteen minutes today? I have to have some blood work done."

"I hope you're feeling okay, that your treatments are helping," Rick replied politely. He wondered when Douglas would start to lose his hair. Chemo often did that.

"Oh, I'm well enough," Douglas replied, clutching his manila envelope. "The blood test is just routine. Now, you know what I'm going to say," he admitted. "Another story! I'm calling this a sort of a fictional memoir," he chuckled. "Lucky for you, this one is longer, so I've made some jumbo-sized chocolate chip cookies for the extra wait."

Nautilus

The nautilus is a pelagic marine mollusc of the cephalopod family Nautilidae, the sole extant family of the superfamily Nautilaceae and of its smaller but near equal suborder, Nautilina. It comprises six living species in two genera, the type of which is the genus Nautilus.

—Wikipedia

Search the internet for "Nautilus" and one gets Wikipedia, and then, the exercise equipment company. *I know he would have liked that name, Nautilus,* Claire thought. She flashed back to reading aloud to her young son at bedtime, how sweet it was. They cuddled up while she read Jules Verne's classic *Twenty Thousand Leagues Under the Sea.* She remembered Captain Nemo's proclamation, "Just remember this: I owe everything to the ocean; it generates electricity, and electricity gives the *Nautilus* heat, light, movement, and, in a word, life itself."

But now she needed a crematorium. The Nautilus Society would do.

Claire and her husband, Brandon, entered the small office housed in a strip mall in Fremont. They barely remembered how they had driven there, still in complete shock.

Thank heaven for cell phone navigation. The receptionist asked them to have a seat in the staged living room until Mr. Arnold Cummings escorted them to the sales office. He was a solidly built, tall man wearing a blue business suit and tie, his expression serious but polite. He shook their hands and introduced himself.

"Welcome to Nautilus," he spoke softly. "Today we will begin the process of taking care of your loved one's remains. Now, your son's name is Sean?" They nodded, numbly. Claire fought to hold back the tears welling up. All day the waves of grief had repeatedly surged over her like ocean surf.

"I assure you, we will make this go as smoothly as possible." He took a ballpoint pen from the cup on the table, detached a form from a clipboard, and placed a folder in front of them while he began.

"Here, at Nautilus, we pride ourselves on a cremation process that is streamlined, knowing how difficult this is while grieving. The first step is to get information about Sean." His voice faded into a drone as he asked for all the data that matters in a civilized society—Social Security number, date of birth, date of death. Where was he born? How many copies of the death certificate will you be needing?

Claire shrugged, thinking, *No copies, because my son is not really dead.*

"You don't have his Social Security number with you? That's all right. You can call it in to me later. Now, copies of the death certificate will be twenty dollars each. How many would you like to order?"

She looked blankly and shrugged her shoulders, "Two?"

"No worries," he assured them. "You can always order more from the county clerk's office. Now, what city and state was he born in?"

"He was born in Mountain View, California," Brandon answered.

Claire shook her head, "No, Palo Alto. Remember? I switched obstetricians after Thomas, then had Sean at Stanford Hospital." Brandon acknowledged it with a nod. Hard to keep the hospitals straight, thirty-eight years later.

"So, the coroner has finished his autopsy, and your son has been transferred from the Santa Clara County Morgue," he explained, "and we have him at our care center, prepared for cremation. Let's go over our package offers so you can pick the services you'd like." He pulled the appropriate sheet from the folder and pointed with the pen tip, "Let's go over our premium package." He read aloud from the flyer:

"This package includes the basic services of the funeral staff, transfer of the body within seller's service area within a fifty-mile radius to a licensed, climate-controlled holding facility and to the crematory facility, completion of the certified death certificate, the process of cremation with alternative container, a choice of a premium urn, delivery of the cremated remains within seventy miles, or mailing of the cremated remains, thirty-five funeral thank-you cards, use of our grief helpline for one year, and the scattering of your loved one's ashes at sea, or in our Nautilus garden."

Claire was thinking, *It must be very hard to be a funeral director, to maintain an air of solemnity while making a sales pitch.*

"Now, with the deluxe package, we will perform a funeral service at our Care Center in Oakland."

"What is a care center?" she asked, while at the same time thinking, *He doesn't need care now.*

"The Care Center is our new funeral site, and the crematorium may be at the same location. Fortunately, our Fremont Care Center has both on the site.

"You are probably wondering how this compares to the basic package," he commented.

She wasn't, actually. She was wondering why her son had to die suddenly from a heroin overdose in the middle of the night, at home, in his own room.

"With the basic package," he continued, a bit more solemnly, "Sean's ashes are placed in the standard plastic urn and you pick up the ashes and death certificate from us."

He scanned their expressions for preferences.

She looked at Brandon, leaned over and whispered, "We can scatter the ashes ourselves. No urn."

Brandon nodded in agreement. "We would also like a viewing of the body before cremation."

"Oh yes, that can be arranged. We can have Sean prepared for a fifteen-minute viewing as if he were in a funeral casket at our Care Center. For an additional charge of course."

"Yes, please add that," Brandon replied.

"OK, so let's go over the final list. So, you'd like the basic cremation with a private fifteen-minute viewing of the prepped body." His pen ticked off the appropriate boxes as he continued, "Without the memento bracelet with your loved one's name? No memorial service by our funeral director? No urn? You did see the wide array of urn choices, correct? You'll pick up the ashes yourself from San Leandro? No ashes scattered at sea?" He scooted back in his chair, and looked up.

"Oh, goodness me. I forgot to mention this. We're in the midst of developing a brand-new service. We can spread his ashes in the Redwood National Forest, with your son's name on an environmentally green plaque at the base of a redwood tree."

He glanced up to check for a possible go ahead, but got nothing. "Okay, moving forward, may I have a credit card for processing your Nautilus contract?" Brandon pulled out the credit card.

"Thank you," the man said respectfully. "I'll step away now to prepare the invoice and get a printout."

Left alone with Brandon, she could finally let go, let grief flood out. Tissue boxes were conveniently placed by the coffee cup full of ballpoint pens, monogrammed with "At Peace with Nautilus." Five minutes later Mr. Cummings returned. They signed the contract. As they stood to leave, he shook their hands once more, adding the customary condolence.

"Again, I am very sorry for your loss. I will meet you at the Care Center next week for your viewing of Sean. Then I'll text you in about two weeks when I have his ashes and copies of the death certificate."

They stumbled out the exit into the blinding California winter sunlight. Claire was wondering why everything was so brilliant on the darkest day of her life. She was wondering why they called it Nautilus Society. What did that have to do with cremation? She wondered if human ashes are as dark as black tar heroin.

She was wondering if she could just curl up and die. At the base of a redwood tree.

Under a blanket of Sean's ashes.

The Black Box

Rick gulped, then carefully placed the manuscript back on the car seat.

Okay, so people overdose all the time. Just call it a tragic coping error. He glanced at his watch. It was already 7:40 AM. He wondered, *what's taking him so long?* Another five minutes passed, and still no Douglas Newton. He was feeling really sick. He hadn't slept enough. He was shaky and his back was killing him. He needed to run another errand before attempting to get to the final technical writing class. He needed that class credit, even if he had to take a pass/fail grade. He was trying to think of what to say about Douglas's sad story. The old man should stick to realistic fiction, but maybe something a little lighter next time. It was almost 8 AM, so where the hell was he?

Rick decided to track him down. He locked the car before heading to the side door of the clinic, looking around for a nurse's station. There were no patients in wheelchairs, no lounge seat stations with IV drips. He saw a line of men, young men, middle-aged guys, old guys, a few women. All waiting in line. Some had black cases, most didn't. Douglas wasn't in that line. A sign on the glass window was posted above the counter:

Douglas brushed him on the shoulder. He held a cotton ball in the crook of his arm, bending it up.

"Sorry, there was a line for the blood tests, too." He motioned with a wave around the room, "Welcome to my world! I'm ready to go now."

He clutched his black case as if it contained gold. As they made their way to the exit, he grabbed a brochure from a magazine stand, handing it to Rick. It read: *Managing Your Opioid Addiction With Medication.*

Rick choked, "Hey! I thought I was giving you rides to chemotherapy!"

"To tell you the truth, I might have preferred cancer to this disease." As they headed out to the Prius, Douglas hoped Rick was ready.

They climbed into the parked car, both silent, Douglas searching for the right way to confront Rick without damaging their relationship. He glanced at him, carefully unlocked the black case, displaying the plastic vials of liquid methadone. Shocked, Rick started the car, slowly pulled out and glanced over at Douglas, waiting for him to explain.

"The first high was like flying into the center of heaven," Douglas confessed with a sigh. "You know, in my entire life I had never felt such calm in my brain. So, I looked for something to help myself. But, you take a hit *just one time.*" He shook his head and frowned.

"In your mind, you think it will be okay. But one hit was one too many, and now a thousand hits will never be enough."

Rick nodded in understanding. "In the beginning you're

paying to get high, so I've heard, and toward the end, you're feeling really stupid because you're paying just to not be sick."

"Yes, and that's for the rest of your life," Douglas added, "unless ... you die from an overdose." Rick took a deep breath. "Or," Douglas delicately went on, "one could decide to try option two, to accept the help of a substitute—naltrexone, methadone, or buprenorphine, synthetic opiates, as a part of medication-assisted treatment, and then therapy for as long as it takes."

For Rick, the revelation was sinking in, that he was like a driver merging onto the "highway to hell" with eternal gridlock traffic and no exit ramp. Staring straight ahead, Rick went silent. He wanted to just get this interfering old man-Yoda-godfather-Jiminy Cricket-guardian angel delivered home. He turned on the radio to drown out any more talk, so he could think. He pulled up abruptly at the apartment complex, tires scraping the curb, parked, and faced him.

"So, were you one of the characters in the suitcase story?"

Douglas laughed, "That damned suitcase! Yes, but that's not the finale. Maybe you could help me with that ending. You know I'm not good with endings."

Rick shut off the motor and leaned forward, resting his head and arms over the steering wheel, saying nothing. He was sweating. He hurt like hell. He might have to vomit. He motioned goodbye as Douglas left his cash tip on the seat and slipped out silently. The radio played the song, "Desperation:"

> Angels catch me, heal me. I release my grip
> Surrendering my soul to the unknown.
> I choose to survive.

The following Thursday morning, Douglas sauntered out to the curb in front of the Monticello Apartments, carrying his case. This time a dark blue Honda sedan was waiting for him.

"Are you Douglas Newton?" asked the Uber driver.

"Yes, but where's my regular driver, Rick Harris?"

"He couldn't make it today. He's just left you a text. I'm Joel. If you are okay with it, I'll take over his rides for a while."

Douglas pulled out his cell phone to read Rick's text.

"I'll be at Mountain Creek Rehab House. I'll text you when I get back in about twelve weeks. Thanks for the stories. Maybe try writing a mystery before I return."

Douglas grinned as he read it. *That* was a good ending! He took a deep breath and climbed into the Honda Accord. "So, Joel, tell me about yourself ..."

Godfather

It was a cool, damp March morning. The spring chill invaded his arthritic knees, but Douglas rocked back and forth on his feet to keep warm. While he waited at the corner, his grey tabby kept him company on the steps. A familiar Prius darted onto Monticello Circle and slowed to a halt, hand waving from the window. Douglas headed across the street, smiling.

"You're back!" Douglas exclaimed, with his raspy smoker's voice. *Douglas looks even older than I remember,* Rick thought. His hair finally had some silver and his shoulders were hunched a bit more, but his eyes were bright. He pulled back a jacket sleeve to point with pride at a nicotine patch on his arm.

"I'm finally letting go of cigarettes!"

Rick smiled, nodded his approval and slapped him on the back. "Yeah, new beginnings for us both. Let's get you to San Jose. As the car headed south on Highway 280, Rick continued, "I finished treatment, I'm making it to Narcotics Anonymous meetings. I'm on buprenorphine for managing my opioid dependency. It's like a low-dose methadone."

Douglas smiled, knowing full well the leap Rick had taken. Detox is an excruciatingly painful and lonely journey through purgatory, where one's recovery must continue amidst a tribe of kindred souls.

Rick continued, "I can drive you today, but sorry Douglas, I might not be able to drive you later, a few weeks from now."

"Oh? That's too bad! Your substitute driver was needing a break from my stories."

Rick explained, "Got an interview for a tech writer position tomorrow morning."

Douglas sat up straight. "Well, that's great news!" He squinted, studying Rick's face intently. "Your eyes look clear. Your skin looks healthier. Are you sure you're ready for an interview?"

"No, not exactly," Rick confessed. "I'm driving you today, but then I'm going home to prepare. I also have to make my NA meeting tonight." His tone was a bit frazzled.

"I'd like to help you." Douglas offered.

"With what exactly?"

"Prepping for the interview."

He hesitated. "I appreciate it, really. But how could you help?" He was thinking the old man had been to a few interviews in his day, but in high tech? And help him pull it together in twenty-four hours? He didn't even drive anymore.

"Tell me about the job."

"It's a good opportunity at a new company, Genovation X. Just an interview, but I have a shot at it with my experience and coursework."

"Trust me. I'm your godfather. Not the Mafia sort. Think of me as your spiritual godfather. Or a straight fairy godfather. I do know a thing or two about the tech industry. I used to work at Apple. To be clear, that was in the 1970s, when wireless phones were the size of Subway footlongs."

Rick felt compelled to accept his help. If twelve weeks in rehab had taught him anything, it was to trust more and talk things out. He felt a twinge of anticipation and hope for the first time in eons. Douglas waited patiently in the car while Rick packed up a duffle bag at his apartment. He fumbled through closets and drawers grabbing interview clothes: a business shirt, khaki pants, and blazer—all business casual. He threw the duffle bag in the back seat.

Douglas double checked his packing before he drove off. "Got your razor? Laptop cord and cell phone cord? Laptop case? Medications? Project samples? Coursework credentials?" He had everything he needed.

Upon arrival at his small one-bedroom apartment on Monticello Circle, Douglas motioned for Rick to set his duffle bag and clothes on the chair and make camp on the couch. While he brewed fresh coffee, he started a simulated interview.

"Welcome to Genovation X, Mr. Harris," he commenced, emerging from the galley with two cups of strong coffee.

"Oh, come on! Rehearsal?" Rick groaned. "We don't need to do this."

Douglas ignored the protest and thrust out his hand. "Shake it," he ordered. "The first impression is made with the handshake. Most people aren't aware of their own energy field. Handshakes are an indicator of your mojo, so show it!" He took a sip of coffee and continued.

"You're applying for the technical writer position, correct?"

Rick nodded. "I graduated from San Jose State with a BA in English. After an internship in technical writing, I accepted a full-time sales position at Ideation in Sunnyvale."

"May I ask, Mr. Harris, why did you leave Ideation?"

"Well, I got sick," he began.

Douglas raised a hand, blurting, "No! You decided to take a year off to go back to school. They don't need to know you were sick," he explained, "but they might learn about it later. Let's hope years later. What they need to know is that you're qualified and motivated." The rehearsal continued.

"What courses did you study this year?"

"I completed two intensives: one in electronics and another in technical writing."

Douglas nodded in approval, then asked, "Why do you think you'd be a good match for Genovation X?"

There it was, Rick the imposter, exposed. He shifted his gaze to the old shag carpeting, stumped. He had no reason why they should want him. There were others better suited, fresh out of college, trained in all the newest technology. He knew he had just blown the interview.

"Cut!" Douglas exclaimed. He motioned to Rick's laptop on the coffee table. "Research the company on the internet."

Rick complied. He began scanning through the material while the aroma of chili and chicken simmered on the stove. While Douglas mashed ripe avocados and chopped up tomatoes and cilantro, Rick jotted notes from various articles. Half an hour later Douglas carried the food on an old plastic tray out to the lanai table.

"Chow time!" he announced, sweeping dust off the chairs. The food wasn't gourmet, but delicious and nourishing. Spicy, but not too hot.

"Hey, this is ten times better than fast Mexican takeout." Rick finished off a third taco with the last of the guacamole.

"Are you ready for a retake of that last question?"

Rick wiped off his chin and grabbed his research notes.

"I read in the *Journal of Engineering* that you're expanding your product designs for all types of computer hardware." Douglas nodded an approval. "I'd be a good fit for Genovation X because I'm blown away by the new innovations in computer devices. I love describing their capabilities. And, I see that your goal this year is to improve your online marketing platform to increase your international base." He stopped to swallow the final bite of taco.

"That's where I excel!" He swallowed and continued, "When I was interning at Ideation, I wrote the white paper for their new product: a keyboard with sensor touch capability that increases anyone's typing speed. I wrote the copy for their website, teaming with the web designers." He paused to open his briefcase and pull out a rumpled packet.

"I'd like to show you some work from those projects."

Douglas gave an approving grin and the interview continued, until he raised an eyebrow and solemnly asked, "But why a year off from Ideation, Mr. Harris?"

Rick flashed back to that humiliating last day at Ideation, passed out in his car in the parking lot. A coworker friend, Jennifer, had rapped on the driver window.

"Rick! Wake up! It's 1:45! You've missed the 12:45 meeting. They're looking for you. Better get back in the office, fast!" She pounded the window again as he nodded off.

"Rick! I'll call 911 if you don't get up now!"

Looking up at Douglas, he took his time forming a fake-it-until-you-make-it response.

"I decided that night courses with a full-time job would take too long, so I changed to a flexible job as an Uber driver so I could finish the coursework quickly."

Douglas gave him a thumbs up, satisfied it was passable. Then he locked eyes with him.

"Mr. Harris, what would you consider your biggest weakness, and how do you compensate for it?" He sat back, explaining, "Yes, guaranteed they will ask you that."

That was the ultimate elephant in the room.

"Well sir," he hung his head trying to hide a grin, cracking up, "to tell you the truth, I've had this rather nasty opioid addiction for the past ten years, and I risked my life and career on a daily basis." He burst into a laugh at the absurd, raw honesty of it.

Douglas joined him. They laughed until they wiped away tears.

When he could finally catch his breath, Douglas went on, "The question is about personal growth. How well do you know your own talents and your weaknesses? How have you learned to compensate for your weaknesses?"

He paused, then solemnly offered, "I'd say you're a master at coping, having endured years of detox, relapse, and recovery. You have patience, gratitude, and you've learned some humility. You just need to articulate how it applies to your career."

He smiled, adding, "Just don't mention the heroin addiction!" Douglas got to his feet. "Why don't you go for a run and think about your response to that? If you head south for three blocks, you'll see the middle school soccer field and track. While you're gone, I'll spruce up your interview clothes."

Rick removed his jacket, his long-sleeved shirt, and threw on a t-shirt. Needle scars on his arms were still visible, but he figured no one would notice them while he jogged. Once outside, he took a few moments to stretch.

Monticello Circle was in a Mountain View neighborhood composed of a hundred slapped-together homes built in the 1950s, most of which would eventually be bulldozed to build new homes. Still, the middle-class suburb was pleasant and peaceful. Mulberry trees lined the streets. The afternoon sun warmed him, but intermittent spring wind gusts sent icy shocks down his back. He jogged along the cracked sidewalks until he reached the middle school field and track. Here he could run laps and think. Images of his own high school surfaced. How he had loved his own high school track! He used to run there to blow off steam when things got tough. It triggered painful memories. Fleeting scenes of arguments with parents, fights with Jeanette. Losing her. A few years later, it was Annalisa. Sweet Annalisa. And finally, Gemma, the love of his life. He would never forget her final words.

"You say you love me, but I never feel you near."

Couldn't she understand it? I couldn't cope without time to decompress. It was asking too much. He remembered the day she packed up and left. Her tearful goodbye, her final embrace full of forgiveness. Then the unbearable pain of watching her walk out.

He stretched and began jogging, pacing himself, finding the rhythm between his stride and breaths. Totally focused on his breath, things began to feel surreal. Was it the pounding from his feet on the pavement or just his heartbeat? He couldn't tell. He surrendered to the burning of his muscles. He realized now that life would always have pain along with beauty. He glanced up at the cerulean blue sky and the canopy of heritage trees over the streets.

He jogged on. The memories and feelings of his past slowly dissolved. No more guilt, regret, and failure, only his beating heart and his lungs filling with air. The air was humming with aliveness, as if each atom was rearranging itself to welcome him into a realm of no time, no space. He jogged on, remembering a favorite rap:

> *Let go of the trap, crawl out of the night,*
> *Hold back the mind—awaken in the light*
> *Let go of fear. Find heaven right here,*
> *Find heaven. Find peace. Find love. Right here.*

Between heartbeats, the pulse of energy permeated his senses. Brilliant sunlight, hum of the air, wind, warm sweat, aching muscles—a synchronized dance. Attuned with that energy, he felt weightless, connected to a vast cosmos beyond the dense track, field, and matter.

So, this is "presence." He jogged on. Ancient memories surfaced, one after another. He remembered now, his lives as a messenger, a soldier, an athlete, a warrior. He had run in desert sands, in marathons across the Greek hillsides, and trekked through ancient coastal forests of lifetimes before this one. Running had always brought him peace. Why had he quit?

He jogged five laps around the track before heading back to the Monticello Apartments. He wondered about Douglas. Why had he taken such a kind interest in him? He figured that Douglas saw himself in him, members of an addiction survivor's club. Even though dizzy from the laps, his heart beat with curious anticipation. He stopped to stretch, gasping for breath, drinking in the sweet, healing energy. The return cool-down walk became the meditative strides of a Buddhist monk. The neighborhood landscape glowed with astral colors: the trees of lime green, the lawns of sap-green velvet. Heaven was right here, even in this nondescript neighborhood.

Douglas was waiting at his apartment door to let him in. "Are you ready to share your weakness?"

Rick gulped water from a bottle, wiped the sweat from his forehead and dropped onto the frayed couch. "Well sir," he began, "I'd say my weakness is resistance. I used to pride myself on meeting deadlines. I worked nonstop, ignoring my own health needs. He checked Douglas's reaction, adding, "I learned that I accomplish successful projects when I balance my career with a healthy lifestyle."

Godfather nodded in approval and slapped his back. "Go ahead and shower, then we'll have a late snack."

Douglas's shoebox apartment was not luxury living, but it was comfortable and clean. Rick appreciated a cooked meal, a hot shower, even a clean towel. Small blessings. He was grateful for his friend and mentor with his nonjudgmental vibe. If his life could be this simple and satisfying, he'd take this deal. He donned his sweats and a clean t-shirt. He found the music streaming channel to tune into some light acoustic guitar while they enjoyed a late snack of turkey sandwiches. They cleaned up the kitchen, then relaxed on the couch.

"Years ago, I had it all. A beautiful family," Douglas began, stroking his cat, "a smart, hard-working wife, a son, and daughter. We took luxury cruises through the Mediterranean. Lived in a four-bedroom home overlooking the Pacific Ocean on an acre of land. Had my own real estate business. Over the course of my addiction, I lost my family, my business, my health, and my self-respect. He sighed, stroking the cat's chin, her purring rumbling louder.

"Still, I'm grateful. When I finally accepted my need for recovery and surrendered my ego, the emotional pain dissolved. I finally found peace. Even happiness. It was there, under all that pride. "And," he grinned, "I have this precious stray cat who has adopted me." From the couch, he sat up and faced his acolyte.

"Don't look back. Stay humble. Don't let one slip put you back in the illusion of separateness. No man is an island. Talk things out."

"But there's the rub. How do you prevent a slip into relapse?"

"I imagine myself bodysurfing."

"Bodysurfing?" Rick repeated incredulously.

"When you're bodysurfing in the ocean, you don't try to outswim the waves crashing on the shore." He stroked the cat's tail and went on. "You learn to work with the waves. You feel the waves surge, then dive deep into them. You emerge on the other side of the crest, just floating and bobbing along in the currents."

"I'm more like the kelp in the tidepools," Rick confessed. "I'm holding fast to the rocks as the waves trash me."

"Let go of fear and allow yourself to feel everything. Every emotion, every physical sensation. Acknowledge and surrender to every joy, disappointment, fear, and pain. All feelings are in the moment. Meditate to focus on the present. You'll realize that you are not your problematic ego." He let the cat leap off his lap.

"How are you feeling about the job interview?" he asked.

Rick shifted on the couch. "A bit nervous."

"You want the job. You're hoping you're the stuff of genius they're looking for. Yeats said, 'Genius is a crisis that joins the buried self in rare moments, to our daily mind.' Genius actually means 'attendant spirit,' being in the invisible care of a spirit. Having been broken by crises in life, we have cracks. Through those cracks you get a glimpse of a new reality. Get beyond your past thoughts, your old self. Let your consciousness flow back into the unified field of the spirit, where energy and love unite everything. That's the key to starting your new life." He paused to let that sink in. "Don't worry about the job interview, Rick. Your life is already genius."

Rick nodded. "We taste and feel and see the truth. We do not reason ourselves into it." He added, "My mother taught me a bit of Yeats."

He excused himself and left for a Narcotics Anonymous meeting. When he returned, his pressed clothes lay out over the armchair, his laptop and cell phone had been charged, and clean photocopies of his projects and recommendation letters were in a folder set atop his backpack.

Crossroads

Rick left at 8:45 AM for the Genovation X interview. He hoped to decompress in the parking lot and check his notes, but cell phone directions took him to the wrong end of Homestead Road, losing him twenty minutes in traffic. He started to sweat, pounding the dashboard. It was already 9:45! Eventually he found the visitor parking lot. He glanced up to find a sticky note Douglas had taped to the car dash: *Remember to breathe!*

Dan Adamson, Genovation's human resources lead, ushered him into his office. They shook hands. Rick managed to relax and smile through the interview. Adamson was impressed with Rick's past work. The interview ended forty-five minutes later.

"Well, Mr. Harris, we'll have to get a background check and follow up on your references. I'll get back to you in about a week. If things check out, you'll be called back for a second interview with our team. The start date would be about two weeks from today."

They shook hands again. Adamson walked him out to the lobby.

As they passed the conference room, Rick did a double take. Rick stopped short of the open doorway and waved to a man with a shock of wavy black hair at one of the tables. The man looked up, squinted, then smiled and stood up, calling out,

"Hey, Rick Harris!"

Rick grinned, turning to Adamson, "I didn't know Colin works for Genovation! We were in classes together at San Jose State!" Adamson smiled, pleased to have an in-house reference.

Returning to his car, Rick leaned back in the driver's seat. He took several more deep sighs of relief. With closed eyes, his life rewound in reverse: Douglas's place, then detox, the Uber lifts, the years of heroin use with withdrawals and relapses, quitting his job, his breakup with Gemma, the college stress. Beneath it all was high school, where he had stood at the crossroads, where choices had been made. Conscious choices he'd made to numb his feelings, believing himself unworthy and alone in life.

Angels lift me back up to life.
I choose to survive ...

He chose now to live with life's myriad of feelings: anxiety, anger, disappointment, pain, passion, and joy. He was worthy of love, simply as a human being. He phoned Douglas.

"Godfather! Yes, think I aced it." He choked up. "Thank you. For everything."

"Synchronicity, son! Now, could you give me Uber lifts until you start the new job? You suggested I write a mystery story while you were gone. I need your feedback again."

"Deal!" Rick exclaimed, "I'll bring the coffee this time, but please could you bring a few of those chunky brownies with the walnuts? And what's the title?"

"*Ashes of the Phoenix.*"

"Sounds intriguing."

"You'd better make those extra-large coffees."

The only thing that is

ultimately real about your journey

is the step that you

are taking at this moment.

That's all there ever is.

Eckhart Tolle

Afterword

I wrote *Uber Lift* to take readers on a journey into the hell of opioid use disorder. The tales are allegories, illustrating the power of addiction. My hope is that the shock value of each story might wake up readers to the dangers of opioid overdose.

In the midst of the Covid-19 pandemic, our attention is on combating the deadly virus. As a result, we're losing focus on the dire epidemic of opioid addiction. The Substance Use and Mental Health Services Administration reported in their 2019 National Study on Drug Use and Health an estimated 10.1 million people nationwide ages 12 and older misused opioids. Of those, 9.7 million people misused prescription pain relievers and 745,000 people used heroin.[1] The Centers for Disease Control and Prevention (CDC) reported that in 2019, there were 49,860 opioid-related overdose deaths in the U.S.[2] The National Institute on Drug Abuse reported that in 2019, 3,391 young people ages 15 to 24 died from an overdose of heroin and other illicit opioids.[3] Many of the opioid overdose deaths are attributed to the street drugs of heroin laced with the synthetic opiate fentanyl. Fentanyl is fifty- to one-hundred times more powerful than morphine.[4] Users have no idea whether fentanyl is mixed into their doses of illicit street drugs like OxyContin and Percocet. They overdose and simply stop breathing.

My son, Kyle, is one who died from an overdose of heroin laced with fentanyl. He was sensitive, well-loved, witty and intelligent. A talented writer and musician, his fault was having an opioid use disorder.

Opioid addiction does not discriminate based on economic class, race, age, or gender. An equal-opportunity destroyer, it kills our sons and daughters, fathers, mothers, and friends, young and old. The resulting social and emotional trauma as well as the economic loss caused by their illness and deaths impact families and communities across the nation. Drug addiction is an economic burden we're all shouldering. Researchers at the CDC estimate that the abuses of prescription opioids come with a multi-billion-dollar price tag, including the costs of "health care, substance use treatment, criminal justice, lost productivity, reduced quality of life, and the value of statistical life lost."[5]

How can we meet the challenges presented by this epidemic? We need to remove the social stigma of this disease. We should educate communities about opioid use disorder, then expand outreach programs to prevent drug addiction in our youth. We need to equip our communities with trained responders, instead of police, in overdose emergencies. We should distribute naloxone (Narcan) kits to reduce deaths by overdose. We should identify and support those at risk earlier, and help those already addicted, with affordable therapy, recovery programs, and medically-assisted treatment. Each of these actions will help save lives.

Proceeds from the sale of *Uber Lift* will be donated to organizations working to raise awareness about opioid use disorder and treatment options. You may contact me with your stories, feedback, and suggestions at rldosskey@gmail.com. Please also visit my blog: yougotthisrecovery.com.

—*Robin Dosskey*

Acknowledgments

My thanks to the following for their generous help: Sara Merryman for her assistance with manuscript revisions; Anne Dosskey for book design; Jim Smyth for the cover illustration; Mary Edwards for proofreading and copyediting; and Susan Weisberg and Sarah Zeltser for their reviews. Special thanks to my husband, Bruce, for his emotional support and encouragement, and for being an enthusiastic sounding board and reader through all drafts of this book. And thanks most deeply to the parents, families, and friends of loved ones who have lost their lives in the current opioid epidemic, and in whom I find solace, support, and the inspiration to channel grief into greater personal and community awareness in this challenging time.

Notes to the Afterword

1 Centers for Disease Control and Prevention, Opioid Overdose: Drug Overdose Deaths, page last reviewed: March 3, 2021, https://www.cdc.gov/drugoverdose/data/statedeaths.html, accessed April 21, 2021.

2 National Institute on Drug Abuse, Drug Overdoses in Youth, March 15, 2021, https://teens.drugabuse.gov/drug-facts/drug-overdoses-youth, accessed April 25, 2021.

3 Centers for Disease Control and Prevention, Opioid Basics: Fentanyl, page last reviewed: February 16, 2021, https://www.cdc.gov/drugoverdose/opioids/fentanyl.html, accessed April 21, 2021.

4 Centers for Disease Control and Prevention, Opioid Basics: Fentanyl, page last reviewed: February 16, 2021, https://www.cdc.gov/drugoverdose/opioids/fentanyl.html, accessed April 21, 2021.

5 Feijun Luo, PhD; Mengyao Li, PhD; Curtis Florence, PhD. Centers for Disease Control and Prevention/Morbidity and Mortality Weekly Report, State-Level Economic Costs of Opioid Use Disorder and Fatal Opioid Overdose—United States, 2017, April 16, 2021; 70(15)541–546. DOI: https://www.cdc.gov/mmwr/volumes/70/wr/mm7015a1.htm?s_cid=mm7015a1_w, accessed April 21, 2021.